The Merc

By

Brother John

i

Dedication

My former father-in-law, Herb Sherburne, was a gifted historian and storyteller. "Partner," as my boys called him, fascinated Nate, Andrew, and me with his tales of his father, grandfather, and The Merc.

I married into the Sherburne family, but my boys are true Sherburnes as well as Bruingtons.

This book is dedicated to Partner (Herb Sherburne) and to Nate and Andrew Bruington, who are also born Sherburnes. It is their history as much as it is Partner's—and that of the many Sherburnes who came before them.

Acknowledgment

Obviously, I'm just the scribe here, while **"Partner" (Herb Sherburne)** is the real author. This is *his* story—and, in a way, his grandsons' story too.

I tell my own tales in my columns and books. I don't have a biography written yet, though maybe someday others will see fit to provide one. For now, you're stuck with mine.

The publishers want my picture (ugh!), but truth be told, it really ought to be *Partner's*.

About the Author

The Reverend Dr. John Bruington, known to most folks simply as Brother John, holds a B.A., a Master's, and a Doctorate, and has spent more than 35 years serving as a pastor across Montana, Wyoming, South Dakota, Colorado, Indiana, and back again in Montana.

Though many believe his cowboying days came before ministry, the truth is that he cowboyed during his early pastoral years, splitting his time between church work and the open range. Those long days riding herd and the honest company of working folks helped shape the plainspoken approach to faith and life that became his hallmark.

He is the longtime author of the weekly Christian cowboy column "Out Our Way: Theology Under Saddle," which continues to run in the Havre Daily Chronicle in Montana. A collection of those writings has also been published under the same name and is available on Amazon.

Brother John's work brings together the ruggedness of the West and the grace of the Gospel—reminding readers that faith belongs not just in church pews, but out on the open range where life and truth meet.

Introduction

In 1977, I was ordained in Great Falls, Montana, as the Assistant Pastor of First Presbyterian Church. Two years later, in 1979, I married into the Sherburne family and became acquainted with their remarkable history on the Pikuni (Blackfeet) Reservation, where the family business, The Sherburne Mercantile, was founded.

Contrary to what some assume, my years cowboying did not precede ministry—they overlapped with my early years as a young pastor. Those long days in the saddle, often wedged between Sunday sermons and mid-week visits, shaped the plainspoken theology and practical faith that would follow me throughout my career.

This is their story.

Prologue

As Joe stepped off the train in Browning, Montana, home of the Blackfeet Nation and reservation, he knew it would be a hard row to hoe. He had worked with the Cheyenne in pre-reservation days and later with the Ponca and Pawnee in the Indian Nations. Indeed, he had been the first postmaster and one of the founders of Ponca City in what became the state of Oklahoma.

He was not the first trader and mercantile owner to come to the newly developed community of Browning, and numerous hopefuls had come before and failed. The resident mercantile traders expected him to fail as had so many others. They had found the "greenhorn" traders often had no idea of how to run a mercantile in Indian Country, and these old timers benefited when the tenderfoot traders went bankrupt. They were able to buy up their stores and supplies cheaply. So, when Joe showed up, the old timers grinned and winked at each other and told Joe, "Build her big." And that is exactly what Joe intended to do.

Joe was no stranger to adversity and hard times. Born in Maine shortly before the Civil War, his father had founded a successful logging and sawmill business, but when he died, unscrupulous lawyers had managed to trick his mother into signing over the business to them. Joe never trusted lawyers after that - and would see others bamboozled and broken by accredited attorneys who preyed on widows- as these vultures had preyed on his mother and him.

Robbed of his family inheritance, Joe set out to support his mother and family by working as a logger - and when the Maine forestry industry began to fail, he moved west, getting all the way to Minnesota, where he continued to work as a logger. But he wanted more - and as the West was opening up, he dared to take the risk to find a better profession. In Kansas, he found a man who owned a mercantile and was willing to make young Joe his apprentice and become a pharmacist. But above all, he was to learn how to trade with Indians. And so it was, while learning to be a pharmacist, Joe also became an "apprentice Indian Trader". The Southern

Cheyenne in Colorado were designated as a good market, and young Joe was sent out to trade with the still "wild" Indians.

As it happened, Joe had a knack for languages and, in addition to becoming fluent in Indian sign language, he also began to learn Cheyenne - a notoriously difficult language for whites to learn. But he did, and he also became proficient in Pawnee, Ponca, and a number of other dialects. Added to this was his personal honor, which allowed him to become a tough trader but an honest one. Indeed, he gained a reputation as "The Honest White Man", which helped him gain the trade and respect of many Native peoples.

In time, Joe set himself up in business and built his own Mercantile and trade center in what was then called "The Nations" [i.e., Oklahoma]. He worked with the Ponca and Pawnee peoples, who trusted him and helped him thrive. In time, he sought to back off from being a trader and, after helping found Ponca City, became the first postmaster. In addition, he saw the rising demand for beef as cattle began to be moved up from Texas to Kansas, and started buying longhorns on his own. The Ponca trusted Joe and granted him property, so he began to build up a large herd and became something of a "tycoon" in the Nations. His herds were large, and he was making money sending them to Dodge and other railheads. And as Oklahoma was closer to these major railheads, his cattle were fresher, stronger, and more in demand than those trailed up from Texas.

Joe had become an important part of the community and the Territory. His ranching was making him wealthy, so the mercantile, pharmacy, and such became less important. But then came disaster. It was called "Texas Tick Fever". It began to decimate cattle herds in Texas, the Nations, and Kansas. Many trail herds were turned back by local officials because so many carried the disease, but it was too late for Joe. Longhorns he had purchased to help build his herd turned out to have the disease, and soon his herd was wiped out. Joe was broken.

But he still had the gift of his reputation as being "the honest trader", his expertise in Plains Indian Sign language, and his ability to eventually learn their language. Cattle were not his destiny, but trading with Native peoples was. So, he got on a train that connected him with the Great Northern which ran through Browning and connected the Hipline of Montana with Seattle, San Francisco, Minneapolis, Chicago, New York, and so forth., and came to Browning with a large amount of cash loaned to him by a widow in Ponca City who knew his gifts, his honesty, and his drive.

He stepped off the train at Browning - and smiled when the locals, expecting him to fail as so many others had done, told him to "build her big" - for that is just what he planned to do. And as the years went by, not only did he succeed, but he bought out many of those who had laughed and thought to take over his store. Thus, Joe - later to be known by family and friends simply as "The Old Gentleman" - created "The Merc", whose legacy 100 + years later remains to this day. This is the Merc's story.

Table of Contents

Chapter 1: Good Trade

Long before the "Old Gentleman" stepped off that train in Browning, other traders and merchants had come to live amongst the Blackfeet and had become an accepted part of the community. They got to know the Blood, Piegan, and Pikuni people with whom they traded, and, of course, the people got to know them. Sometimes that could make things difficult, for in the culture, it was understood that no one was perfectly honest when it came to trading. Both sides tried to get the best of the other but if you ended up on the losing end, you had to keep quiet about it. If you made a 'bad trade' and complained, the word went around, and you were no longer someone with whom the people would do business. If you were in the mercantile/trading business, that would be fatal to all future enterprises.

Now as it happened, although the U.S. Government had set up the largest military post in the nation at Fort Assiniboine [near modern day Havre] some miles to the east of the Blackfeet and west of the Gros Ventre and Assiniboine lands, imposing "peace" on the Plains between the tribes, raiding parties from various reservations still set out against their traditional enemies. If an Army patrol caught them, the raiders would be severely punished, and the whole community would face difficulties with Washington. Nevertheless, small raiding parties set out from time to time to steal horses and perhaps count coups against neighboring tribes. The threat of the Pony Soldiers simply made it an even greater feat in the eyes of the young men seeking to make a name for themselves.

Now, one trader in the area, we will call him "Hank", was doing a brisk business amongst the Blackfeet and looked to become an important man in the territory. He was also a bachelor who looked to change his marital status and had a sweetheart in the riverboat town of Fort Benton. Fort Benton was the end of the line for steamboats that plied the Missouri, and just south of there, one ran into the impassible Great Falls that had stymied the Lewis and Clark

1

expedition for so many weeks. Thus, Fort Benton was the "big city" of the day, and after a long and brutal Montana winter, Hank was ready to head downriver to his sweetheart.

Now the Missouri is many miles east of the Blackfeet country, and in those days, without many roads, the fashion was to load up some horses and trek cross-country to the river. There, you cut large piles of firewood which the steamboats needed for fuel, and traded for passage. Hank and his friend "Bob" packed a horse with supplies, gifts and various items to bring a smile to Hank's loved one's eyes, saddled their own steeds and armed themselves with good rifles and pistols as well as a saddlebags filled with ammo, dried beef, some whiskey, and whatever else they could fit in, and headed for the river.

They made good time, cut piles of wood, and soon enough flagged down a steamboat headed for Fort Benton. Trading the wood for passage, they loaded their horses and themselves aboard the boat and headed south on the "Mighty Mo". Unfortunately, the Missouri is not always cooperative and especially in the spring when the rains fall and shift the landscape, sandbars pop up that have to be dealt with. Sometimes the skipper could avoid and manage to steer around them, but other times the steamboat hit and got stuck. Then it could take hours and sometimes days to get free and continue the journey. This was one of those times, and the boat was stuck good and tight.

It had been a long winter, and Hank was eager to get to Fort Benton and his beloved "Sarah", so he and Bob unloaded their horses and rig and headed out cross country through the famous "Missouri Breaks", sure they would arrive at their destination long before that steamboat would. Ah, but they were wrong, for they were not the only ones roaming the area. Hidden amongst the cottonwoods and the brush was a small raiding party of Blackfeet coming back from a successful raid in the Gros Ventre area. As Hank and Bob's trail led them down a deep arroyo, they suddenly found themselves surrounded by a dozen Blackfeet warriors decked out in warpaint and fresh off a successful raid. Now the biggest problem facing all parties at that moment was the simple fact that, as a major trader amongst the Blackfeet people, not only did every warrior know Hank and Bob, they knew every one of them.

Some of the young men, eager to keep going but aware that Hank and Bob could tell the Army who they were, demanded that they kill Hank and Bob. After all, they were not "of the people'" and there were other white men with whom they could trade. It was a wild country with many wandering bands of various tribes, and in such an isolated area, their bones would bleach white long before anyone found them. No one would know it was the Pikuni who killed them.

Fortunately for Hank and Bob, the leader of the raid was a wise older warrior with a sense of humor, and he had a better idea. Instead of killing the traders, he suggested they "trade with them". So he had a trading blanket set out, invited Hank and Bob to sit, and suggested a trade. Pointing to their horses, rifles, pistols, supplies, and all, he began a lengthy speech on traditional fashion, the gist of which was that "the Pikuni looked upon Hank and Bob as brothers and fellow warriors. Therefore, it 'grieved' the Pikuni to see their brothers mounted on such poor specimens of horseflesh and so poorly outfitted in such wild and dangerous country. Therefore, because the Pikuni loved and honored their brothers, they would trade a fine and worthy steed fit for great warriors for their poor and useless horses, weapons, supplies, and all else they carried.

Despite the fierce visage of these scowling warriors in their war paint, Hank could see the laughter in the eyes of all but the youngest raiders who had really hoped for blood. The war chief asked if Hank and Bob agreed, which of course they did, and the chief declared it was a "good trade". And so, sometime later, Hank and Bob, mounted on an extremely old and worn out horse the raiders had used as a pack horse armed only with their pocket knives continued their journey while the raiders dashed back to the reservation in high spirits of both their successful raid in the Gros Ventre, but also their "good trade" with the white traders. Should either tell the authorities what had happened, no Blackfeet [and likely no other Indian] would ever trade with them again.

Indeed, in exchange for their lives, it had been a "good trade".

Many years later, Hank shared this story with the Old Gentleman, but added, "The rule works both ways - and as I had to keep silent about what had happened and who did it, I never forgot. And believe me, over the years of doing trade, I got even with every one of them!"

Chapter 2: Wyatt Earp

Back in the day, when the "old gentleman" was a "young" gentleman, he came to settle in Kansas for a time. It was there he apprenticed as a Pharmacist but also learned to become a trader with native peoples. He often took wagon loads into Colorado and met with the Southern Cheyenne, but that's a story for a different day. The railroads had come west, and Kansas had become the focal point of the Texas trail drives. Places like Dodge, Ellsworth, and Wichita had grown up and prospered as the "end of the trail" destinations for these big herds, but they also had become centers of saloons, brothels, and wild cowboys. The town marshal's office was usually located near the cattle pens and on the "wrong side of the tracks". The marshal's job was less about law and order and more about keeping the cowboys, gamblers, con men, and hookers away from the decent folk who lived in the "good part of town".

The "law dogs", as some called them, were hired bullies and ruffians who were no more welcomed nor honored than any of the other riff raff on the wrong side of the tracks, and were looked down upon as a necessary evil by the "good citizens". They were expected to stay on their side of the tracks with the other scum unless summoned by the Mayor or City Council. As the saying went, "if you want to keep the dogs out of your yard, you put a bigger, meaner dog at the gate." That, in essence, was the role of the town Marshal.

Of course, back East, where western mythologies written by the likes of Ned Buntline had become popular, names like Buffalo Bill, Wyatt Earp, Bat Masterson, and others had become "heroes" to youngsters in New York and Pittsburgh and the like through the Buntline dime novels. But those who lived in those cow towns saw things differently. While Buntline, and later Hollywood, would create an image of the wild West that "thrilled" the ignorant and set up Buffalo Bill, Pawnee Bill, and other "Wild West" showmen in lucrative theatrical portrayals of a fictional West designed to bilk the gullible folks back East and Europe; folks like "the old gentleman" who actually knew and lived amongst some of these "famous and popular figures" knew better.

In his later years, sitting around the pot-bellied stove in the Mercantile, the "Old Gentleman" would recall his days in the "wild west" portrayed by Buntline and other fiction writers and remind his listeners that Wyatt Earp was scum. He also reminded them of cowboys, drifters, and gunmen whom the Earps feared, and while Buntline never knew or at least never mentioned them in his popular novels, the folks in Dodge, Ellsworth, Wichita, and numerous other cowtowns knew them. And the "old gentleman" would laugh and share how he had seen Wyatt and the other Earps back down and step off the sidewalks and into the mud to let such men pass.

Ned Buntline was a New Yorker who sold western fiction to New Yorkers. He mythologized the West and made a fortune selling myths to gullible Easterners. Later, one of his creations, "Buffalo Bill" Cody, would create a Wild West Show that would take the East and Europe by storm - but would always be a joke to the real Westerners. So it was, on cold winter nights in Montana, gathered around the pot-belly stove during an "Alberta Clipper", folks would eat crackers, sip hot coffee, and laugh as the latest Buntline novel was read. "The old Gentleman" was not the only one who had been there and knew the truth of the Buntline fictions. Wyatt Earp was no hero to those who rode the Texas trails into Kansas. Many of them had gone from riding the Chisholm Trail to moving herds along the Bozeman Trail. The "old gentleman" was not the only veteran of those long ago days, nor the only one who had both met and despised Wyatt Earp and other Ned Buntline creations. There is a Plains Indian sign that was often used by both Native and white folks in the region. It is a gesture in which the speaker seems to be throwing something down, and that "something" is understood as excrement. The meaning is "I throw #@%* on it." As they laughed in the Merc at the Buntline novels and the idea that Wyatt Earp was anything more than a bully and a fake, they made the Plains Indian sign in unison, and laughed even harder.

Chapter 3: Levi Byrd - The Good Land

Originally, the reservation was owned by the tribe as a whole, but there came a time when tribal members could buy specific sections for themselves and their posterity, and Levi Byrd was one of those fortunate ones who was able to stake out his claim to prime farmland. Of course, he had an advantage over many others in the fact that he had known of the rich soil in a certain area on the Rez long before the tribe and the US government opted to allow individual tribal members to buy specific sections of the Reservation as private property. Sometimes being a "cowboy" pays off, even if you are an Indian!

Cattle drives were still a part of the West when Levi was a boy, and most of the Reservation was open range. Levi, like many other youngsters [including the old Gentleman's son, Frank], cut their teeth working roundups and on cattle drives in Montana. Now, as it happened, Levi was a bit too young to be an actual cowhand on his first cattle drives, and so signed on as a cook's helper. The cook for the big trail drives was an older white man who had lived a good deal of his life on the open range and became something of a celebrity for his cooking skills when the roundup and trail drives took place. Levi was something of an apprentice to him, and the old man took Levi under his wing.

Not only did "Cookie" teach Levi how to set up camp and the chuck wagon, but he also shared with him valuable insights about the trail they traveled as the herds were driven to the railhead for shipping. One spot on the trail was especially important for a young Levi Byrd, for "Cookie" showed him that it was one of the most fertile spots on the trail. Over the years, "Cookie" had peeled potatoes and tossed the skins off into the brush, and in one area, those old skins had not rotted away, but had become a new potato crop because the soil was so rich. Where "Cookie" had tossed potato skins away was becoming a rich farmland where new potato plants had begun to grow and prosper. Levi never forgot.

7

When the Tribe opened the land for homesteading by tribal members, Levi staked his claim in that spot "Cookie" had shown him and became a successful and rather wealthy farmer. As "Cookie" had shown him, the land was fertile and year after year, Levi's farm produced bumper crops. Levi became something of a local legend due to his success. He liked to go to an old tree on the land that had been the site of many a cook's wagon on the trail drives. Levi and "Cookie" worked - pointing to the soil and saying that it was here he peeled the potatoes that would sprout and grow in later years and prove that Levi knew good land when he saw it.

Chapter 4: Frank, Charlie, and George

Although the "Old Gentleman" was a Pharmacist, Trader, and Businessman, like many others in the area, he was also a rancher. It will be recalled he had been a successful and wealthy rancher in the "Territories" [later called Oklahoma] before the Texas Tick fever wiped him out, but the disease didn't seem to be around Montana. Now he had married in Oklahoma and had a son, Frank, who would later recall the land rush ceremonies he witnessed as a toddler when the federal government officially opened the territory to homesteaders.

After going up to Montana and getting things settled, the "Old Gentleman" brought his family up to create their Browning home. Boys grew up fast in the West in those days, and young Frank began doing the work of a grown man when he was still a boy. Thus, at age 10, Frank was given the responsibility of taking a herd of horses from Browning to Great Falls. It was a long journey, and before the days of the automobile, there were few roads and much of the trip was cross-country. Now his father hadn't been much older when he had left Maine and traveled to Minnesota as a lumberjack and later to Kansas to become a trader. He had told Frank of his experience taking trade goods out into Colorado to trade with the then-hostile Southern Cheyenne. Especially harrowing was the "Old Gentleman's" first journey into Cheyenne territory when he had run across the bodies of several scalped white men who had been "porcupined" [filled with arrows from a Cheyenne war party]. Years later, when he had mastered Plains sign language and had become fairly fluent in the Cheyenne tongue, he discovered he had been trading with the very band of Cheyenne who had killed those white men. They explained that the whites they killed and scalped were "surveyors" who always preceded road builders … and where the roads were built, large numbers of homesteaders followed. There had already been too many clashes between whites and the Cheyenne, with the Cheyenne usually on the losing end [see the "Sand Creek" and "Washita" massacres]. But traders were different

9

and were welcome. Yes, they had seen and secretly followed the young trader as he made his way across their lands, deemed him harmless, and welcomed him. Indeed. In later years, they honored him and invited him to come ride with them on buffalo hunts, which he eagerly did.

Times had changed, and the hostilities ended and living amongst the Blackfeet as an honored member of the community, young 10-year-old Frank had nothing to fear from any native bands as his father had on such a journey; but that is not to say he had nothing to fear. For even with the end of the so-called "Indian Wars" there were shrill rustlers, robbers, and gangs aplenty in the "big open". Even to this day, the Montana State Police sport the old vigilante symbol [3- 7-77] on their squad cars. The reference was to the Vigilante warning that thieves and crooks faced the grave [3 feet wide, 7 feet deep, 77 inches long] if caught. Indeed, one of the first men caught and hanged by the Montana vigilante was a corrupt sheriff who worked with gangs robbing miners. Police were rare in the area, so folks had to look out for themselves and Frank was a crack shot.

But I digress. Frank made the trip alone with the herd, driving them over several days to the rail yards in Great Falls, where he was to collect on delivery the already agreed upon sum the "Old Gentleman" and the buyer had negotiated. But when Frank arrived, seeing that Frank was "just a kid", the buyer tried to lower the price and badger the boy into accepting less than the agreed-upon amount. But the buyer didn't know Frank, nor, apparently, did he know Montanans.

At the stockyards that day were two important figures in Montana history, Long George Francis and Charlie Russell. As most folks know, Charlie Russell was by then a well-known, famous, and wealthy artist. Like Frederich Remington, Russell had become a major figure in the art world and especially Western art. Unlike Remington, however, Charlie not only lived in the West but had worked as a cowboy. His portrayals of the Native tribes and cowboys had gained him a huge following back East and a lot of political clout in the country. "Long" George Francis was perhaps not as well known outside of Montana, but in the state, he was a force to be reckoned with. Sometimes called "The Gentleman Outlaw," he had gained a reputation for being another one of that special breed you didn't want to cross. Being on both sides of the law at one time a law officer in Havre and at other times a suspected rustler and leader of an outlaw gang, George demanded and got respect.

As it happened, George and Charlie were friends and shared old times as they were looking over a shipment of cattle at the stockyards when they heard the commotion between Frank and the horse trader. Curious, they eavesdropped on the confrontation between Frank and the buyer. The buyer, because Frank was only 10, was trying to "jaw the kid down," as he put it, and intimidate him. But Frank was having none of it and loudly made that plain. Frank was not one to bully [as some "tough: folks up in Browning would learn over the years] and refused to back down. He knew what his father had offered, and the buyer had accepted, and refused to accept anything less.

George and Charlie liked Frank's "spunk" and decided to "back his play". They let the buyer know they thought "the kid" had every right to expect the buyer to uphold the deal he had made with "the old gentleman "[whom they also knew]; and they made it clear they would stand with Frank. Neither George nor Charlie made any threats, but they didn't have to. You don't want to challenge Charlie Russell, the famous artist and Montana's most famous celebrity, and you definitely do not want to face Long George's, the "gentleman outlaw's" wrath. The buyer backed down and honored the terms he had agreed to. And so Frank collected the agreed amount, thanked Charlie and George, and rode back to Browning without further incident.

As for the horse trader, legend has it he left town shortly thereafter to seek easier prey than young Montana cowboys and their fellow

Montanans, who tended to frown on liars, cheats, and those who would try to prey on youngsters.

(Working horses at the corral, carrying on the Sherburne tradition of horsemanship.)

(Visiting with the horses at the home corrals, continuing the long lineage of Sherburne stock work.)

Chapter 5: Frank's First Trail Drive

Although Frank had herded a cavvy of horses from Browning to Great Falls, the real test of his competence as a cowboy lay ahead. Though the railway was connecting Seattle to Minneapolis and points in between, the stock yards were still many miles east of "Chief Mountain" and required many of the same old ways that cowboys had been using doing it back in the Chisolm and Bozeman trail days. Now, in those days, there was usually one older steer or cow that was something of a leader for the drive, and sometimes that steer could be less than cooperative.

Frank had been practicing with his rope, and some of the older trail herders were encouraging and egging him on. Sometimes the lead cow or steer needed a reminder of who was in charge and one of the tricks the old timers showed Frank was how to toss a loop over the misbehaving cow or steer, and with a good roping horse, suddenly pull tight as your cow pony took off in a different direction, and toss the misbehaving bovine on its back. Usually, after such a lesson, that steer or cow never gave the cowboys any trouble again.

Now, as the herd was being brought down from the Chief Mountain area, Frank had been given the special privilege of riding point and helping direct the herd instead of riding drag, [riding in the rear, pushing the herd and eating dust; the position usually reserved for tenderfeet and the least skillful like yours truly cowhands.]

Now, as it happened, there was a particularly ornery steer in the herd that was giving Frank trouble. After a long spring and summer in semi-open range, this steer had become "rangey" as the saying goes, and was not at all cooperative. He refused to stay with the herd and kept trying to bolt. When Frank went after him, the ornery critter would become angry and often charge him. It was time to teach him a lesson. So Frank unhooked his rope from his saddle, swung out a good-sized loop, and tossed it over the steer's head, pulled it taut, dallied the rope around his saddle horn, and then spurred his pony full bore diagonally away from the offending bovine. As expected, as the rope snapped tight, the maneuver threw the steer off balance and flipped him on his back. Unfortunately, it also broke his neck.

Needless to say, the trail boss was less than pleased and noted the trail was not a rodeo arena, that trailing cattle was a job, not a sport, and loudly bewailed how Frank's "fancy roping" had cost them all by reducing the number of cattle they would be able to sell when they finally got to market. Indeed, he quired, would they have ANY cattle to sell if Frank didn't shape up? That night, and for a few days afterwards, the daily "chuck" was beefsteak, which the crew enjoyed almost as much as they loved "hoorawing" Frank for the rest of the drive.

(Preparing and handling saddle horses, much as Frank and earlier cowhands would have done).

Chapter 6: Loading The Cattle Cars with George and Curly

Arriving in Havre, the main shipping area for Northern Montana. Frank and the others pushed the cattle into the loading pens, and when the trains arrived, they began the hard and dirty work of loading. Usually, one of the unlucky cowboys from the trail drive ended up working the chutes, standing in the pen on foot, driving cows up the ramp, and into the cattle car. This day, the job fell to George a rather unpopular fellow with the crew and also something of a mystery. Despite what you may have seen in the movies and on TV, few cowboys actually wore guns on the trail or in town. Indeed, most towns had very strict laws about firearms, and the cowboys had to surrender their weapons when they came in from the drive. But out at the chutes and the stockyard, it wasn't technically a "town", so a few, like George, still wore their "irons".

Now no one knew for sure, as George had joined the drive as an outsider back in Browning, but George claimed to be a dangerous man. Frank assumed it was true, but ole Curly, who had never liked George, did not. So on that day, as George was down in the corral on foot, sweating and fighting obstinate cows as he sought to get them to go up the ramp into the cattle cars, Curly sat on the top rail of the paddock, laughing and making fun of George.

Curley was something of a vain man and had bought fancy sheepskin chaps for the drive and was wearing them that day as he sat "in the opera house seats' [top railing of the corral] hoorawing [making fun of] George. And George was getting tired of it. "I ought to shoot you and fight off the fence," George yelled at Curley. Curley laughed and said, "You never shot anybody and just bought a marked gun, you liar!"

Well, it went on and on between the two of them, and all the cowhands were enjoying the show, especially as George was getting

17

angrier and angrier as Curley egged him on. George began to turn red with anger as Curley made fun of him, and the rest of the crew started joining in. "I ought to shoot you off that fence," George started yelling, and Curley just laughed louder and suggested George couldn't hit the broad side of a barn from inside with a handful of gravel. And everyone else laughed.

Well, George simply couldn't take it any more and drew his pistol and fired a shot in the air. Nobody was really sure George had shot at Curley, but Curley flew off that fence and landed on the ground. And then everyone noticed those sheepskin chaps of his were no longer white, but were rapidly turning red. George noticed too and went white. And then he put his pistol back in the holster and jumped over the fence and high-tailed it out of town. It was later rumored he had stolen a horse and ridden over the border into Canada to escape the sheriff and the posse sent after him. But nobody ever caught him, nor did anyone ever try, for you see, Curley was still alive.

What had happened is that when George fired the shot, the bullet never came anywhere near Curley, but the sound of the gun going off had caused him to jerk up and fall off his seat on the top of the corral fence. He had fallen backwards, hit his head, and knocked himself out when he hit. As for the red, it was not blood, but scarlet colored liniment he had bought for his arthritis that he had been carrying in his back pocket. When he fell off the corral fence and knocked himself out, he had also broken the bottle of liniment, and as it seeped out, it strained his chaps and vest.

When Curley came to shortly after the incident, he discovered his beloved sheepskin chaps and white wool vest were ruined. George never knew the truth, and folks say he remained a fugitive in Canada for years before he learned the truth, but even so, Curley never forgave him for ruining those pure white sheepskin chaps of which he was so proud.

(A quiet moment between horse and handler—part of everyday ranch life on the Highline.)

19

Chapter 7: Pack Saddle Sam

At the end of the trail, the cowhands got their pay based on the sale of the cattle, and that included Frank. Though still a mere boy, he got paid like all the others and, like all the others, headed for the south side of the tracks where the brothels and saloons flourished. It was also where the con men hung out, waiting to pick off the foolish and naive cowboys who came with gold in their pockets to celebrate the end of the trail. One of the best and most successful was a scammer known as "Pack Saddle Sam".

When a herd came in, Sam and his crony would wait for the crew to come into a saloon and then set up their trap. Sam's crony would come in first, pretending he was a fellow cowboy from a different herd, and strike up a conversation with other cowboys. He would share the trials of the trail and the inadequacies of the cook, and all the other things cowboys complained about. He might even buy a few drinks as a "fellow cowhand" and seek to gain their trust as one of them.

Then "Sam" would come in. Sam always dressed like a "dude from back East" and arrived in the saloon shortly after the train had pulled in. Pretending to be from New York or Philadelphia, he would come in in a suit and tie and do all he could to give the impression of being a greenhorn tenderfoot. His "partner", the guy who pretended to be one of the cowhands, would lead the way by ridiculing the "dude", goading the cowhands to laugh at the "tenderfoot". The "dude' would declare he rode horses in Central Park and therefore could ride anything the cowboys rode.

Now, in every remuda, there was at least one horse that never fully accepted a rider, and the "bronc rider" each outfit hired had to ride it down before it was of any use. Even so, most professional bronc riders got tossed along the way, and it became a matter of pride to have a horse that could not be ridden in the herd. You begin to see the plot.

The "stranger" would egg on the 'dude' and suggest the horses the cowboy rode were far too "fiery and snuffy" for a dude … and of course the "dude" would be "insulted and demand he be allowed to ride anything the cowboys could throw at him. Indeed, he would say he had ridden horses in New York's Central Park and thus could ride ANY horse with ANY rig; and to back it up, he laid $50 in gold pieces on the bar. The man's "secret partner" would back the bet and encourage all true cowboys to kick in their own coins to shut this dude up.

Many of the crew took their pay and laid it on the bar when the bet was made by the "dude," as the unknown cowhand egged on the others to accept the bet that this dude could and would ride any horse with any saddle the cowboys could provide. Frank sought to get on it as well, but the trail boss grabbed him and pulled him back. "Son," he cautioned Frank, "That's 'Pack saddle Sam' and he is going to take every dime on the bar before tonight's over. Hold onto your money and watch."

Indeed, the stranger suggested, once the bet had been made, that as the dude had not specified what sort of saddle he would ride with, an old pack saddle would be provided. No seat, no stirrups, and no balance. And he encouraged everyone to raise the stakes to really destroy the dude. But as the trail boss knew and Frank was to learn the dude was actually a world champion bronc rider who had perfected riding on a pack saddle with a rangey pony. And so, as Frank's trail boss had warned him, "Pack Saddle Sam" rode down that jughead and scooped up the entire month's wages from the crew except for Frank and the trail boss's coins, who both had not made the bet.

Over the years, Pack Saddle Sam arrived on the train when the herds came in, always dressed in a fancy suit and looking like a New York dude. His partner, wearing trail clothes, came on the same train, went to the area saloons and scouted out the most likely suckers, then set them up for the "dude's" act. The trail boss had lost most of his wages as a youngster when he rode on his first trail drive, and

21

delighted in watching others learn the same lesson. But he took pity on Frank and warned him before Pack Saddle Sam took Frank's wages, and fortunately, Frank trusted his trail boss. He went back to Browning with his pockets full of cash and the wisdom of a lesson learned and never forgotten.

(Gentle groundwork in the corral, reflecting the patience at the heart of true horsemanship.)

(Family working together with a young horse—a reminder that ranching is a shared heritage)

*(Teaching and training in partnership, echoing the generations
who learned their skills on Montana soil.)*

Chapter 8: Glacier Park

The US Government began to set apart national parks, and Montana had two of them. Yellowstone was, of course, a major attraction with "Old Faithful" and the other natural phenomena, but Glacier with its Grizzlies and wild, untamed beauty was not to be ignored either. The Federal government sent a survey team to lay out Glacier National Park, and one of the locals hired to help the surveyors was none other than Frank Sherburne. Frank was the packer, cook, and guide for the surveyors who laid out the boundaries and created the first maps of the park, and often guided them to areas they needed to survey. But Frank was raised in the area and knew most of it intimately. The Blackfeet feared the interior as "the Land of the Great Moose," who they claimed caused the great winds that came along the Rockies when he flapped his ears. They also feared the White Snow Owls, who congregated on a hill outside town and where, as a joke, Frank, in his later years, set up a Ku Klux Klan burning cross to show his disdain for the racist group that was so powerful in the early years of the 20th century. Having run into a great Snowy Owl in the Rockies many years later, I can attest to the size and disturbing mannerisms of the bird when one comes across one in the middle of the night. I get why the Blackfeet feared the bird and thought they were the ghost of relatives come back to haunt the region.

Frank had guided and packed through the region since his youth, once even being a guide and cook for an old-time train robber who had just gotten out of prison. He had been hired to take the ex-con on what was supposedly a fishing trip to an obscure lake in the mountains. Frank set up camp outside an old cabin they found and spent the next few days fishing. Surprisingly, the man who hired him did not fish but spent his time in the area around the cabin doing who knows what. A few days later, the man said he had had enough and wanted to go back to Browning. Frank noticed that the man's saddlebags were strangely bulging and after they got back home, the man took off for Canada and was never seen again. Later, he learned that the man had been part of a train robbery years before, and although he had been caught and sent to prison, the stolen money had never been recovered. Suddenly, those bulging saddlebags took on a new meaning.

Back to more recent times, Frank packed the horses and led the surveyors about the area as they created the maps and boundaries for the proposed Glacier Park the Federal government was establishing. Although the Old Gentleman and the Sherburne Mercantile were well known in the region by that time, it was Frank who gave Sherburne Lake its name. The surveyor had just finished the job at the lake and turned to Frank and said, "Hey, kid! What's your name?" "Frank Sherburne" was the reply. And so the man wrote "Sherburne Lake" on the map, and thus it became and remains to this day.

Chapter 9: The Wrong Ammo

After World War 1, Army surplus stocks were often distributed to Federal agencies, including the Reservations. Government hunters received rifles and ammo originally meant to be sent to France, and the quality was usually top-notch. Certainly, none of those folks hired to deal with problematic bears in the new national park complained, and one such hunter was especially delighted when given a new Springfield 1903 30-06.

Now the area around the park is cattle country, and sheep were also being introduced, so given the wild nature of Glacier, it was not surprising that predators often came around and caused all sorts of damage to herds and flocks on the Reservation. Ranchers and herders went about armed with rifles and defended their livestock as best they could even when Congress declared some species to be "protected". Indeed, most folks in the area practiced the "3 S Rule" [Shoot, Shovel, Shut up]. Bears. Wolves, coyotes, and cougars wandering outside the park boundaries often "disappeared," and Game Wardens seldom knew anything about it. But now and then, some critters seemed to figure out they could escape the rancher's wrath after attacking their herds and flocks by retiring into the Park. When it became clear that this was happening, the government hunters were contacted and sent into the Park to hunt down and eliminate the offending creature.

There was a grizzly bear who had made it a habit of regularly decimating cattle in a certain area - not killing one or two for food, but seemingly killing dozens for sport. The ranchers could track him into the Park, but by law, they could not go further. Only a licensed government hunter sent by Park officials had the authority to track down the offending "Ursus Horribilis" within the Park boundaries and eliminate the problem.

So it was that a Blackfeet hunter, we'll call him "Arthur", was hired by the Park and called in. He was well known for his tracking skills,

27

courage, and being a crack shot. Arthur was called into the Park Superintendent's office, given a new Springfield and several boxes of ammunition, and sent to track down and eliminate the problem. Arthur had dealt with many a bear before and so was not overly concerned about this one. Indeed, he even took his young son with him in order to teach him some of the skills of a tracker and hunter. They arrived at the rancher's spread, who showed them the tracks from the latest incident, and then proceeded to enter the Park and begin the hunt.

It took some time, but eventually Art and his son picked up a fresh trail of this particular bear and began the hunt. By this time in history, most bears had come to fear man, but in the protected Park area, many had lost that fear, so when Art found the bear, it did not run off but began to act aggressively. Art dismounted and told his son to stay on his horse then walked calmly towards the bear with his new Springfield in hand. The bear reared up, and Art took aim and fired. The bear was hit, but did not seem to be badly hurt just enraged. It dropped to all fours and began racing towards Arthur. Arthur fired again and again, hitting every time, but the bear kept coming. Screaming at his son to ride off, Arthur calmly aimed and fired over and over again, but the bear never stopped coming. Only when the bear was a mere 3 feet or less from Arthur did it finally drop and die. Arthur later said he was able to touch the dead bear with the barrel of his rifle; it had gotten that close.

Puzzled at why the bear had gotten so close despite being hit so many times with what would have normally been fatal shots, Arthur noted the bullets had not expanded or tumbled after entering the bear but had passed straight through. Checking the ammo box, he discovered the Government had issued him "armor piercing shells" useful in warfare perhaps, but not against a grizzly. The killing shots had come when one of the bullets hit the bear's spine and broke its back, and a second shot, when the bear had rolled, hit the heart. All the others had passed straight through, no doubt painful, but not fatal. The next time Arthur went out for the government, he checked his ammo.

Chapter 10: Corrupt Lawyers

As may be recalled, "The Merc" adventure did not begin in Montana, but many years before in Maine. The "Old Gentleman" was but a youth when his father died. His father had been a successful businessman in the logging industry and had even built a saw mill as part of his business. Unfortunately, when his father died, a local lawyer came around and managed to persuade the widow to sign papers which, in the end, transferred all the property to the lawyer and left the widow and her family penniless. That is why the "old gentleman", as a youth, ended up having to walk to Minnesota and ply his trade as a logger in order to support his mother.

Years later, as a grown man in Browning, he saw corrupt brothers the Conrad brothers for whom a town in Montana is named - pull the same fraud on the widow of Two-Guns White Calf on the Reservation. The old widow, who did not speak or read English, was pressured by these brothers to sign a paper she did not understand, which legally turned over her late husband's land and property to them. The Blackfeet nation had allowed members to buy sections as personal property, and Two-Guns, the last hereditary chief of the Pikuni branch of the Blackfeet nation, had built a respectable ranch and cattle herd over the years. But when he died, these corrupt white men came and, like vultures, decimated his estate and left his family penniless.

Perhaps because of his own history dealing with such crooked liars and cheats, the old Gentleman made it a personal point of order that he would never lie or cheat another human being, as his mother and Two Gun White-Calf's widow had been cheated.

At any rate, over the years, the various tribes [Cheyenne, Crow, Blackfeet, Assiniboine, Chippewa-Cree, and others] began to refer to the Old Gentleman as "The Honest White man," and his trading business grew. In fact, his reputation was so widespread that when

29

Chief Joseph of the Nez Pierce was defeated and captured in the Bear Paws mountains of Montana, a number of his personal items were given to the Old Gentleman.

Unfortunately, years later, when Frank went to college in Washington at Gonzaga University, those items that the Old Gentleman had donated to the school were stolen by "Not so honest white men", i.e., school officials who stole the artifacts and sold them off to collectors. The "Honest White Man" apparently was indeed a rarity. In ancient Palestine, a small edifice was discovered that had been erected to honor "an honest tax collector". Such a person was so rare that the Jews of the nation commemorated it with a memorial. Perhaps one day there will be a similar monument erected to the "Old Gentleman". If, during the Roman domination of Judea, an honest tax collector had been found, perhaps the Blackfeet and other tribes would consider a similar monument to the "Old Gentleman"- commemorating an honest white man who was as rare in Browning as an honest tax collector was in Roman-controlled Judea.

Chapter 11: A Rattlesnake at the Barbershop

Frank grew up in Browning, which was a small town in Montana by most standards, and so naturally was well known. "The Old Gentleman" had been quite an important personage in his day, being elected postmaster and one of the founders of "Ponca City" in Oklahoma territory days, and over the years, as "the honest white man" and a solid businessman, had gained a good deal of respect and local prestige via the "Sherburne Mercantile." As Browning grew, many looked to "the Old Gentleman" as one of the original founders, to which he always replied with a laugh, "Hell! I rode the train into town!"

Although times changed and the days of trading were replaced with basic everyday commerce, the Sherburne name was still respected and honored. Frank, though born in Oklahoma, was considered a "native son" to the area, and even when "The Merc" was replaced by the Sherburne Hardware Store, the legend of the Merc remained. Thus, it was not surprising that the folks in Browning admired and elected Frank as Mayor of the town.

Now, although the days of the "Wild West" were past, there were still some reminders of the "old days". One such reminder was an old alcoholic former gunslinger we will call "Bill". In his day, Bill was considered a dangerous man, and in the local saloons, folks gave him space, for he was always armed with a well-used Colt revolver that had three notches carved in the handle for the three men he had killed along the way.

Bill was almost always drunk, and when he was "in his cups," his mind was not always rational. So it was that one night at the local hotel, Bill had come into the barbershop demanding a shave, and had almost immediately drawn his gun and started screaming "Snakes!" and started shooting up the shop. The barber ran for his life, the sheriff was called, but promptly resigned his office and tossed his badge away, so it all came down to Mayor Frank.

So Frank came to the hotel barber shop and peeked inside. Bill was no stranger to him [for Browning was indeed a small town in those days] and called him by name. "Bill, it's Frank. What's the problem?" Bill, with the hammer drawn on his .45 Colt, sat in the barber chair and answered, "Snakes, Frank! There's a big rattler after me herein the room!" And with that fired another round. Frank was no teetotaler, but certainly knew the signs of the "D.T.s" Bill exhibited. So instead of trying to "disarm and arrest" Bill. Frank played along. "You're right, Bill - that IS a big rattler! Stop shooting at it and let me get him!" And with that, Frank came into the room with a stout club of firewood and went past Bill to the wood stove where many of Bill's shots had been aimed. He went behind the pot belly stove and started swinging the club behind it and pounding the floor while, exclaiming all the while, "Take that, you S.O.B.!"

Bill stopped shooting and leaned forward as Frank went through the charade, and Bill lowered his gun. "Got him," Frank cried triumphantly! And Bill sank back into his chair, relieved, and promptly fell asleep. Frank took the pistol out of Bill's hands and summoned the deputies who had not resigned as had the cowardly sheriff, and escorted him to the town jail to sleep it off. But this is not the end of the story.

Bill was not the only town drunk in those days, but a woman we shall call Sally was also infamous for her public drunkenness. Bill and Sally met and drank together, but the amazing thing was that they BOTH wanted to sober up for each other. And so it was, they began to court each other and actually stopped getting drunk. Indeed, when Bill proposed and Sally accepted, they made a promise to each other to stay sober from that point on … and to the surprise of nearly everyone, they did.

Chapter 12: The Drunk Pianist

Montana winters are dark and cold, and while we do get the "Northern Lights" from time to time, the Alberta Clippers and below-zero weather make life hard at times. Even so, life goes on, and folks adapt, and so a regular part of winter was the local dances held at the Mercantile. In the days before radio, TV, and the internet, local gatherings were a critical part of life in the winter. The old Gentleman, and later Frank, made sure a part of the warehouse was set apart for winter dances each year. The pot belly stove was fired up and the area cleared so there would be room for couples [and would be couples] to meet, dance, and court in the darkest days of the years.

Now the "Merc" was like a modern Mall in the sense that "one-stop shopping" was critical for the folks on the Highline. That said, it is important to know that the successful mercantile had to offer far more than even the largest Mall of modern times. The MERC handled nearly every category of items, from "soup to nuts" and beyond. At the Merc, you could not only buy clothes, groceries, hardware, liquor, chickens, geese, and feed, but also things like automobiles [when they first made their way into the area], pianos, and even coffins. That sets the stage for today's tale.

"Hank" was a marvelous pianist and was in demand when the winter dances were held. Unfortunately, Hank was also a bit too fond of alcohol and, for all his talent at the piano, was a known drunk. Even so, when the winter dances came around, he was in demand; and so it was one cold February, he staggered into the Merc, ready to get things rolling for that evening's dance. Now, by this time, the Merc has several outbuildings where excess goods were stored, and in one of them was an upright piano fresh off the train for a local rich family. It had not yet been picked up and delivered, so it was set aside in the warehouse for the evening's entertainment. "Hank", as drunk as ever and carrying his whiskey flask with him, came to tune it up for the evening's festivities. He

33

asked and got the key for the warehouse as well as a kerosene lantern to both light his way to the warehouse and illuminate the keys and his musical scores.

Now the "Merc" not only sold automobiles, wagons, and pianos in those days, but also coffins, and contracted with the local mortician to supply the need. As it was winter and freezing cold, the mortician was not overly concerned about embalming corpses, especially those of the local native population, and so tended to just place the deceased body in a coffin and wait until the ground thawed enough to dig a grave. So open coffins containing the bodies of dead men and women were not unusual at the Merc and on the Rez. Thus it was that "Hank" was practicing on the piano in a warehouse, took a few extra nips of "redeye" and, stumbling in his drunkenness, fell face forward into an open coffin in the warehouse and came face to face with a dead Blackfeet chief whose family was waiting for the thaw to bury him.

Now, A.A. suggests several steps towards sobriety, but I guarantee falling into an open coffin with a newly deposited corpse is one that will not be ignored nor brushed off. Certainly, up on the Rez, this man's family was more than willing to suggest that such an event would immediately grant sobriety and the likelihood of remaining sober from that point on.

Chapter 13: The KKK and Owl Hill

Frank was a man with a sense of humor, but also a man who had little patience with radical groups. In the late 20's and early 30's, the Ku Klux Klan was a major political entity in the USA, even up in Indian Country. While few blacks lived in the area, the prejudice of the KKK was still a powerful political force, and Frank was not well pleased that a number of people in the area had become supporters of the movement.

Now, on the outskirts of town, there was a hill with a few trees that attracted Snow Owls every year and among the Blackfeet, like most plains Indian tribes, the owl was feared as a harbinger of death. It was said that if the "owl called your name," you were about to die. It was also believed by many of the older warriors that the Snow Owls that tended to flock to and roost on this particular hill were the ghosts of dead warriors come to haunt the tribe and bring judgment on the living. Thus, "Owl Hill" was to be avoided at all costs, and anyone or anything associated with it was cursed and evil. As a white man, Frank had no fear of owls, but as the son of "the Old Gentleman" and a man of honor himself, Frank felt the KKK was an abomination. As a long-time citizen of Browning, he was well aware of the Native superstitions, and as a man who detested the KKK's open racism, he decided to do something about it.

Thus it was that Frank built his own large cross, hauled it up on Owl Hill, and one night set it afire. This was a clear sign to the KKK in town that they were not welcome. Indeed, the native peoples understood the symbolism and that the fact that the cross was burning on Owl Hill made it clear to the locals that the KKK was evil and to be avoided.

Chapter 14: A Man Who Turned Adversity into Profit

Outside of Helena is an area called "Confederate Gulch". It got its name because during the War Between the States, when both Union and Confederate prisoners of war were dying from starvation, abuse, and various diseases, there were uprisings of the Sioux and other tribes out west. Mr. Lincoln, who hanged Sioux leaders in Minnesota when they rebelled against the Federal government, decided to offer "rebel" prisoners the opportunity to escape the Union death camps if they would swear allegiance to the Federal Government and serve as troops out west to fight against Red Cloud, Crazy Horse, Sitting Bull, and others who challenged the authority of the Government. Many of those "Galvanized Yankees," as former Confederates sent west to fight Native tribes were called, ended up in Montana. Now, as it happened, some of them did a little prospecting, and a major gold strike was found in 1864 by Horse Creek. Thus, the area was christened "Confederate Gulch." Over the years, other prospectors came to pan for gold and dig in the region, and a small community was created that continued well into the 20th century.

In modern times, with the automobile, telephones, and the railroad, the need for the "one stop shopping" Trading Posts like "The Merc" ceased to be practical, and so, like the others, closed its doors. Thus it was that Frank switched over to a hardware store business and continued to be a successful businessman as well as Mayor in Browning. But his love adventure never ceased, and the Confederate Gulch area drew him to invest in a cabin along the creek where he and son, Herb, could pan for gold as well as fish for trout. And so it was that a young Herb learned of the tale of the paraplegic millionaire.